Stargirl Academy

Ava's
Sparkling Spell

VIVIAN FRENCH

WALKER
BOOKS

Stargirl Academy

Where magic makes a difference!

HEAD TEACHER
Fairy Mary McBee

DEPUTY HEAD
Miss Scritch

TEACHER
Fairy Fifibelle Lee

TEAM STARLIGHT

Lily

Madison

Sophie

Ava

Emma

Olivia

TEAM TWINSTAR

Melody

Jackson

Dear Stargirl,

Welcome to *Stargirl Academy*!

My name is Fairy Mary McBee, and I'm delighted you're here. All my Stargirls are very special, and I can tell that you are wonderful too.

We'll be learning how to use magic safely and efficiently to help anyone who is in trouble, but before we go any further I have a request. The Academy MUST be kept secret. This is VERY important…

So may I ask you to join our other Stargirls in making The Promise? Read it – say it out loud if you wish – then sign your name on the bottom line.

Thank you so much … and well done!

Fairy Mary

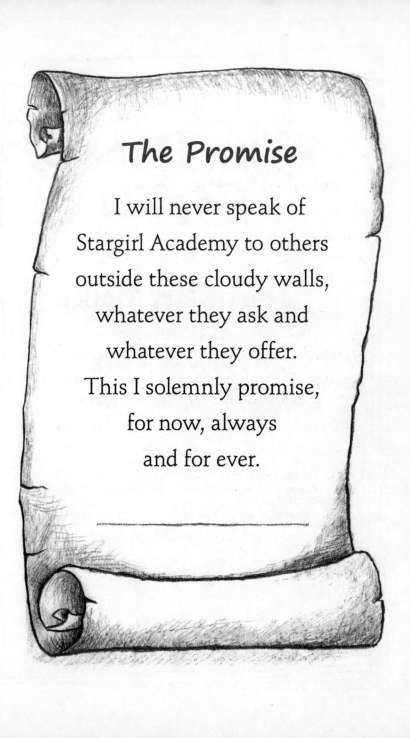

The Promise

I will never speak of
Stargirl Academy to others
outside these cloudy walls,
whatever they ask and
whatever they offer.
This I solemnly promise,
for now, always
and for ever.

_____

The Book of Spells

by
Fairy Mary McBee

Head Teacher at

The Fairy Mary McBee
Academy for Stargirls

◆ ◆ ◆

A complete list of Spells can be obtained from the Academy.

Only the fully qualified need apply. Other applications

will be refused.

Sparkling Spells

Sparkling Spells are to be undertaken with
care. They can, however, be remarkably
effective if used in the correct manner.
Misuse of these spells is not to be thought
of; any such behaviour will lead to severe
loss of privileges.

Sparkling Spells include such spells as:

- Copying actions and behaviours
- Confusing magpies intent on stealing small shiny objects
- Unblocking drains

Hello!

I'm so pleased to meet you! My name is Ava Evangeline Chan, and I live above a café. It's a good thing I do, as my mum is a dreadful cook — almost everything she makes ends up burnt because she's always reading, and she doesn't notice when the kitchen's full of smoke. Dad loves cooking, and he's brilliant, but he gets home late from work, so we have to put up with burnt baked beans (YUCK!). When I very first went to Stargirl Academy and found out we could help people, I thought of Mum at once ... but then I worked out that the person I'd really be helping was me. So when it was my turn to choose I chose Lily.

The Academy used to be called The Cloudy Towers Academy for Fairy Godmothers. Fairy Mary is the head teacher, and she's brought it up to date, so now it's called The Fairy Mary McBee Academy for Stargirls — and that's us! Girls just like me and you. But we aren't proper Stargirls yet. We have to win our stars first and we do that by helping people. Each time we do a good deed a star lights up on our magic necklaces (I love mine — it's really pretty!) and shines for ever. I've got three shining stars so far, and guess what? When I've got six, THAT'S when I'll be a proper Stargirl.

Lily is one of the other girls in my team, together with Madison, Emma,

Sophie and Olivia. We're best friends now. Before I went to the Academy, I didn't have many friends; only lovely Little Val and Tallulah from Café Blush...

And that's where I'll begin.

Love, Ava xxx

Chapter One

The café underneath our flat is called Café Blush, and it's run by Little Val and Tallulah Sweet. It's the prettiest café for miles and miles; inside it's a lovely rose pink, and there are flowery pictures on all the walls. Little Val and Tallulah often stop me when I'm running past the door to give me a huge chunk of the most delicious cake or a carton of yummy soup. We're really good friends. They're much younger than Mum, so they're like the big sisters I've always wanted and I tell them everything – well, almost everything. I've never told them about Stargirl Academy. I'm sure they could keep a secret, but I

had to promise faithfully that I wouldn't tell anyone, and a Stargirl always keeps her promise.

 16

Don't you think it's difficult to keep a secret from people you really like? Every time I see Little Val or Tallulah, I want to tell them about the Academy and how I have five new friends in my team – Team Starlight. And I've been dying to tell them about Melody and Jackson too. Melody and Jackson have their own team, and sometimes they're horribly grumpy – but Fairy Mary McBee (our head teacher) says we shouldn't judge people just because they don't smile all the time. I try hard to think she's right, but it isn't easy.

Another thing I want to show Little Val and Tallulah is my magic star. It's on the end of the little finger on my left hand and it glows. So if the light goes out on our stairs (which it does quite often) I don't feel frightened any more. I used to be scared that something horrible was going to jump out at me from the shadows, but now I see my tiny star shining, and I feel fine. All of us Stargirls have got one; Fairy Mary gave them to us on our very first day. When we learn a new spell, we have to point with our little fingers, and then the stars twinkle really brightly. We've learned a Floating Spell and a Solidifying Spell (a Solidifying Spell makes things heavy – even feathers!) and last time we learnt a Sliding Spell.

We're only allowed to use the spells while we're in the Academy or when we're on a Stargirl adventure. I did once try and see if I could make Mum's handbag float up in the air, but it didn't work. On the other hand that might have been because she had four or five books stuffed inside,

and even the very best Floating Spell wouldn't have been strong enough!

But you don't want to hear about my mum's handbag. It's Stargirl Academy that's exciting. In fact, it's SO exciting that sometimes I think I must have dreamt the whole thing. But then I remember Fairy Mary McBee and Miss Scritch and Fairy

Fifibelle Lee, and I know that I couldn't have made them up. They're too magic.

Who'd have thought I'd meet three real Fairy Godmothers and be invited to train to be a Stargirl? But that's what happened. Whenever I get a Tingle in my elbow (that's the special sign) I know I'm going to spend another wonderful day at the Academy...

And my elbow tingled on the first Tuesday of the holidays...

Chapter Two

Because I was on holiday, I didn't get up all that early. I wandered into the kitchen and found Mum eating burnt toast and marmalade and dropping crumbs all over her latest book.

"M'ph," she said. "Hello, poppet." And then she actually looked up, and I knew at once that something was wrong. "You might want to pop down and see Val and Tallulah, and try to cheer them up. They think they're going to have to close the café."

"WHAT?" I stared at her. "WHY?"

Mum shook her head. "I don't know the details. I bumped into Val late last night and she was crying so much I couldn't catch what she was saying. Something about not enough customers and not being able to pay the rent."

I didn't wait to hear any more. I grabbed my keys and rushed out of our flat, and just as the front door banged behind me and I headed for the stairs, I got a Tingle.

"Ouch!" It was really painful, and I rubbed my elbow. My mind was whizzing – what should I do? I absolutely loved going to the Academy, but my friends were in trouble ... should I see them first? But then I thought, maybe it's meant! Maybe I can help them! And I remembered something important. One of the most extraordinary things about going to Stargirl Academy is that you come back at EXACTLY THE SAME TIME AS YOU WENT!

I know. It sounds impossible. I guess that's magic for you. If I went to the Academy at ten o'clock in the morning, we'd have a whole day of learning spells and having adventures ... but when I got back to my own home it would STILL be ten o'clock in the morning!

I hurried down the stairs and by the time I got to the bottom step I was surrounded by thick mist. When I opened the street door, there was the Academy door right in front of me, with swirling cloud covering the rest of the building. I opened it, and marched inside ... and nearly flattened Fairy Fifibelle Lee, who was doing some kind of weird dance in the hallway.

"Oops! I'm so sorry," I said, as I disentangled myself from her floaty scarves. "I hope I didn't hurt you."

"Not at all, darling." Fairy Fifibelle twirled herself round and smiled at me. "I was just practising a dear little spell that I'm hoping to teach you later. It's enormous fun – I think you'll love it!"

"I'm sure we will," I said politely. "Erm … what is it?"

Fairy Fifibelle held up her arms and did another twirl. She does that a lot, and sometimes it makes me feel quite dizzy … but this time something seriously weird happened. I found that I was twirling too – even though I didn't want to! Fairy Fifibelle saw the expression on my face and she laughed.

"See? SUCH fun. It's a Copying Spell! But don't tell the others. I want it to be a lovely surprise!"

"I promise," I said, and I hurried up the corridor to the workroom where we have our lessons. As I went, I wondered if a Copying Spell could stop Café Blush closing down … and I had to admit that it seemed very unlikely indeed.

Chapter Three

I walked through the door – and stopped dead.

The workroom has cupboards and shelves all the way round the walls, and every shelf is piled high with books and bottles and strange-looking bits and pieces. The cupboards underneath have always bulged – but now it looked as if they'd exploded. The doors were wide open, and the floor was a sea of paper, bits of string, boxes, bent wands, ancient old books and heaps and heaps of rusty pins. My friends Madison and Lily and Emma were sitting in the middle trying to put the books into piles, while Miss

Scritch – our deputy head teacher – stood over them. She was looking even grimmer than usual.

"Good morning, Ava!" Miss Scritch said as I stood and stared. "Perhaps you'd like to help your friends?"

"What happened?" I asked.

Miss Scritch folded her arms. "It appears that Madison was suffering from an excess of curiosity."

Madison straightened her spectacles and flashed me a beaming smile. "I only wanted to see why the cupboards were so bulgy," she said cheerfully. "I could hear them groaning, so I opened a door – and a million trillion things fell out."

"And now we're trying to sort everything," Emma added. "But I'm not sure we'll ever get it all back."

I thought she was probably right, but I didn't say so. "Why are there so many pins?" I asked.

Miss Scritch sniffed. "When this was The Cloudy Towers Academy for Fairy Godmothers, there was a great demand for pins. Ladies of a certain age often need to pin up their hems. And from time to time, the waistbands on their skirts become a little too tight."

I couldn't help smiling at the thought of Fairy Godmothers bursting out of their clothes, and Miss Scritch gave me a

sour look. I decided I'd better try and be helpful, so I bent down, picked up an old battered box and gave it a quick shake to see if anything was inside. It fell apart and thousands of tiny white feathers fluttered into the air. Immediately we all began to sneeze – Miss Scritch more than any of us – and Fairy Mary McBee came hurrying in from the sitting-room next door, with Scrabster, her old dog, at her heels.

"Goodness me! WHATEVER is going on?" Fairy Mary asked. "What a terrible mess!

Oh! I haven't seen those feathers for years and years and years – they must be left over from the cloak we made for the Swan Princess." Her face suddenly screwed up and she sneezed the most enormous sneeze. "ATCHOO! Oh, dearie me. I remember now ... we never used them, did we?"

Miss Scritch was holding a small lace handkerchief to her nose. "We didn't use them because they'd been infected with a Sneezing Spell ... one of Fairy Fifibelle Lee's, if I remember correctly!"

"Atchoo!" Fairy Mary sneezed again, whipped out her wand, and waved it. The feathers swirled into a heap, then tucked themselves neatly into an open bag. The bag snapped shut, and all the other things on the floor arranged themselves into neat piles before stacking themselves back in the cupboard ... and the doors swung shut with a *CLICK*. There was no sign of the mess except for a few scattered pins that hadn't quite made it back in time.

Fairy Mary beamed at us. "I really must thank you – you've done a good deed. That poor old cupboard's been needing a tidy up for a long time now."

"Excuse ME, Fairy Mary!" Miss Scritch was looking like a thundercloud. "Madison was responsible for this mess and she should have cleared it up!"

Madison stood up. "It's true, Fairy Mary," she said. "It was me that opened the cupboard. It looked as if it was just about to burst. I'm very sorry. I should have asked."

Our headmistress nodded kindly at

Madison, then gave Miss Scritch a long, cool stare. "Don't you think curiosity can be a good thing, Miss Scritch?"

"If you say so, Fairy Mary." Miss Scritch's mouth was a thin, disapproving line. "I just hope Madison's curiosity doesn't cause any more trouble. We've wasted quite enough time this morning. Shouldn't the other girls be here by now?"

I'd been thinking exactly the same. Olivia and Sophie weren't usually late; I hoped they were OK. With Jackson and Melody, you never knew; sometimes I wondered if they were late on purpose, just to show us how cool they were.

Fairy Mary pulled a small gold watch out of her pocket and glanced at it. "They'll be here any moment," she said calmly. "Lily, dear, just pick up those pins for me and put them in a drawer. I don't want Scrabster treading on them."

Chapter Four

Fairy Mary was quite right. She'd hardly finished speaking before the front door banged and we heard footsteps. First Sophie and Olivia came hurrying in, then Melody and Jackson sauntered after them.

When Melody saw Lily carefully picking up the pins, she raised her eyebrows. "Those don't look very magic," she said. "Rusty pins? What are they for?"

"They fell out of the cupboard," Emma explained, as Melody and Jackson sat down at the big table in the centre of the workroom.

"Really?" Jackson sounded even more bored than usual. "What a strange place

36

this is. We found Fairy Fifibelle Lee
dancing in the hallway. Maybe she needs
a few pins. Her scarves always look as if
they're just about to fall off."

"She's practising our spell for today," I said, then realised what I'd done. "Oops! I promised I wouldn't tell!"

"A Dancing Spell?" Jackson gave a heavy sigh. "Like that's going to be of any use to anyone."

I didn't answer. I'd already said too much. Instead, I opened the drawer for Lily so she could put the pins away. I was still wondering about Café Blush and Little Val and Tallulah Sweet. What would I do if they closed down? And what would *they* do? It's such a lovely place ... but now I thought about it, it had been rather empty recently. A new café had opened up the road; maybe people had started going there instead? I didn't like the new place. They never said hello, or made people feel welcome, but they did sell very cheap cake.

I tried to remember when I'd last seen a queue outside Café Blush. It always used to be buzzing with people waiting for a seat or to buy a cake or a bag of buns, but over the past couple of weeks there'd been lots of empty tables when I popped in to see if they wanted any help with clearing up—

"Penny for your thoughts, Ava." It was Olivia. She always notices if someone is unusually quiet. It might be because she's very quiet herself; she never chatters on the way that Madison and Emma and I do.

"I was thinking about these friends of mine," I began, but Madison interrupted.

"Ava! Are we REALLY going to learn a Dancing Spell? DO tell!"

Luckily for me, Fairy Mary McBee heard

her and began to laugh. "Maybe one day, Madison, but not today. Could you ask Fairy Fifibelle to come in, please?"

Madison was burning with curiosity, but she did as she was told and Fairy Fifibelle came floating into the workroom.

"Darlings!" she said. "Today is such a very special day! You're going to learn a totally wonderful Sparkling Spell!"

I looked up in surprise. I was sure she'd told me we were going to learn a Copying Spell. Fairy Fifibelle saw me, and gave me a dazzling smile. "It's so confusing. There are *lots* of Sparkling Spells, you see, and the Copying Spell is the one you'll learn today. It sounds boring, but it's fun when you can do it." She pointed at Jackson. "Jackson, dear, would you be very kind and do a cartwheel?"

If looks could kill, Fairy Fifibelle Lee would have fallen over right there and then. "I don't do stuff like that," Jackson growled.

Fairy Fifibelle didn't seem at all upset. She turned to Lily instead. "What about you, Lily?"

Lily went very pink, but she stood up, took a deep breath and turned the

neatest cartwheel I'd ever seen ... and as her feet swung through the air, they left a trail of red and blue glittery sparkles behind her. It looked like the very best kind of Catherine Wheel!

"WOW!" I said. "I wish I could do that!"

"But you can, my petal!" Fairy Fifibelle held up her arms and—

It was CHAOS!!!!

We couldn't stop ourselves; every single one of us suddenly felt we absolutely HAD to do a cartwheel! Chairs fell over, the table rocked, the air was so thick with sparkles we could hardly see – and we were a tangle of heads and bodies and arms and legs as we crashed into each other.

"ENOUGH!" It was Fairy Mary and she must have waved her wand because in one tiny, lickety-split second there we were, sitting down again. Our hair was sticking up on end, our cheeks were flushed, we were puffing and panting – and most of us were laughing as we rubbed our bruises. Jackson wasn't, though. She and Melody were scowling horribly.

"That wasn't funny," Jackson said. "My arm really hurts." She glared at Olivia. "You kicked me!"

Olivia's sweet and kind, and the most unlikely person to hurt anyone on purpose. She looked really upset as she apologised. "I'm very sorry, Jackson. I really didn't mean to."

"I've a good mind to go home right now this minute." Melody pushed her chair back. "This isn't about learning to help people. It's just plain stupid."

Fairy Mary McBee gave the table a sharp tap. "My dear Stargirls, I do apologise. That was most unfortunate." She looked across at Fairy Fifibelle, who was hovering anxiously in a corner. Even her floaty scarves were looking droopy. "Fairy Fifibelle, what were you thinking?"

45

Fairy Fifibelle shook her head. "I got carried away, Fairy Mary. It's such a useful spell, but I should never have asked Lily to do a cartwheel."

Miss Scritch gave one of her most disapproving sniffs. "It's only useful when used correctly," she said sharply. "In fact, I'd say it could be dangerous. I don't think these girls are anywhere near ready for something so sophisticated, as anyone with any sense would realise." And she sniffed again.

"That is TOO much, Miss Scritch!" Fairy Fifibelle Lee positively bounced out of her corner. "I would like to make it clear that I considered the choice of spell most carefully before I came here this morning!"

For a moment, I actually thought Fairy

Fifibelle was going to shake her wand at Miss Scritch, but Fairy Mary tapped the table again.

"My dear fellow fairies! Please! No lasting harm has been done, so let us move on. It must be time for our morning break. What would you like, girls? Hot chocolate, as usual? And I have a new recipe for a truly wonderful coffee cake... But first, can I make sure you are all feeling better? No more bumps and bruises?"

Jackson rubbed her arm in a meaningful way and glared at poor Olivia, but she didn't say anything. The rest of us looked hopeful. The Stargirl Academy hot chocolate is truly wonderful ... although I do think the hot chocolate at Café Blush is even better.

"Please let me provide marshmallows

47

and chocolate flakes as a little extra treat," Fairy Fifibelle begged. "Just to show how sorry I am for upsetting you all."

Miss Scritch gave her a suspicious glare, but Fairy Mary smiled happily. "Of course," she said. "The girls would enjoy that very much. And afterwards you can continue teaching the Sparkling Spell ... and I'm sure you'll try a different approach this time."

Miss Scritch muttered something under her breath.

"Did you say something, Miss Scritch?" Fairy Mary asked. "No? That's splendid. Here we are, then!" She waved her wand and several trays floated down to the table.

Chapter Five

This time, the hot chocolate was better than ever. I don't know if it was the marshmallows or the chocolate flakes or both together, but it really was delicious, and Fairy Mary's coffee cake was so incredible that every slice was gone in minutes. There weren't even any crumbs; Scrabster sniffed hopefully in between the chair legs, but there was absolutely nothing for him.

"If Café Blush sold this cake they'd have queues out of the door," I thought, and I put up my hand. "Excuse me, Fairy Mary, I don't suppose I could have the recipe for your coffee cake, could I?"

"Of course you may," Fairy Mary said. "Remind me before you go home."

Emma giggled. "We shouldn't have eaten it all! We could have copied it with the Copying Spell!"

Fairy Fifibelle Lee shook her head. "It wouldn't work, my darling; it only works with people."

Lily's eyes opened very wide. "So will we be able to copy each other? Like, have two Madisons?"

Fairy Fifibelle laughed. "That's not what I meant, either. Oh, silly me! But it'll be clear as day once you start practising."

I could tell by the way Miss Scritch was stabbing her wand at the mugs and making them thump onto the tray that she was still cross. When she sent the trays flying off to be washed they went

so fast I didn't even see them go, but I did hear an ominous crash in the distance. Fairy Mary raised her eyebrows, but she didn't say anything.

"Now, my darlings." Fairy Fifibelle Lee settled herself in a chair at the end of the table. "Let's begin. Lily, would you pick up your pencil, twist it round and then put it down again? Thank you. Now,

Emma, use your star finger to point at Madison. Concentrate very hard, and imagine her picking up her pencil exactly the way Lily did."

Melody frowned. "You didn't point your finger."

For a second, Fairy Fifibelle Lee looked annoyed, but she managed to give Melody a smile. "Dear, darling girl! Always so observant! But I am a Fairy Godmother with many, many years' experience. You are just beginning. Emma, my sweet, do carry on."

Emma screwed up her eyes and pointed her star finger at Madison.

Nothing happened.

"Let me try," Jackson said. She stared at Madison, her star finger outstretched. Three sparkly blue stars floated round

Madison's head, and she gave a funny little gulp and picked up a pencil. She twisted it exactly the way Lily had done, then put it down.

"WOW!" Madison said. "That was really REALLY weird! I couldn't help myself!"

Jackson looked pleased. "Some people have a gift for magic." She glanced at Emma. "And some don't."

Emma bit her lip. "I bet I can do it," she said, and she pointed her star finger at Olivia. A moment later, Olivia was twisting a pencil round just as Madison and Lily had done and – just for a moment – sparkles were shining in her hair.

"THERE!" Emma beamed. "See? I did it!"

After that, we all tried to make each other copy different things, and sometimes it worked and sometimes it didn't. I managed to make Olivia giggle exactly the way that Sophie does, and Lily magicked me and Madison into sneezing an enormous, sparkly WOOCHOO!!

"Can I try?" Olivia asked, and she made

Emma sneeze three times in a row.

But I couldn't make anyone sneeze at all. "Well done, Olivia," I said. "You're much better at this than I am."

Jackson heard me, and she leant over and whispered in Melody's ear. Melody nodded, and pretended to fall off her chair with a scream and a bump, but when Jackson pointed her finger at Olivia, nothing happened. Jackson tried again and again, until at last Fairy Fifibelle noticed.

"What are you trying to do, dear heart?" she asked.

"Nothing," Jackson said sweetly. "Just a little experiment."

Melody looked surprised. "Come on, Jackson. You were trying to make Olivia fall off her chair, but you couldn't do it." She turned to Fairy Fifibelle. "WHY couldn't she? Jackson's brilliant at spells!"

Fairy Fifibelle put her head on one side. "Perhaps Jackson can tell us why?"

"I've absolutely no idea," Jackson said, and she looked at her star finger. "OH! What's happened? What's happened to my finger?"

Jackson sounded so upset that Fairy Mary came hurrying. "Have you hurt yourself, dear?" she asked.

"My star isn't shining any more," Jackson told her. "Look!"

Fairy Mary stopped smiling. "What were you trying to do, Jackson?" she asked, and there was a chill in her voice that made me very glad she wasn't talking to me.

Jackson opened her mouth, closed it again and stared at the floor.

Fairy Mary looked at the rest of us.

"Can any of you suggest a reason why Jackson's star has faded? And why she couldn't make the Sparkling Spell work?"

I think we all knew the answer, but we didn't like to say. There was a nervous silence before Jackson said in a small voice, "I suppose it's because I was being mean. That's why my star's faded." She looked up at Fairy Mary. "But it will come back, won't it? I didn't mean to hurt Olivia." She rubbed her arm. "Even though she did kick me."

Fairy Mary was still looking serious. "That was an accident. You'll have to be more thoughtful in future, Jackson. My Stargirls are carefully chosen, but you do have to earn your place here too."

Jackson turned to Olivia. "Sorry."

"That's OK," Olivia said. "I really, REALLY didn't mean to hurt your arm."

Fairy Mary McBee nodded. "Thank you, Olivia. Thank you, Jackson. Oh, and Jackson...? Could you please fetch the Golden Wand? It must be time for the Spin."

We all watched as Jackson carefully unhooked the Golden Wand from its place on the wall and laid it on the table. It's always a very special moment when we have the Spin; you can actually sense the magic hovering in the air. When the wand stops and points at someone, it never feels as if it's happened by chance ... that person has been chosen, even if they don't know why.

We pulled up our chairs and I held hands with Olivia and Sophie as Fairy Mary set the wand spinning round and round. The room grew shadowy and the wand glimmered in the darkness. There was a golden glow on everyone's face as we waited to see where it would stop.

"Spin, spin, spin," Fairy Mary sang softly. "Who will choose? Who will it be? Whose destiny will change today? Spin, wand, spin."

The wand went on spinning for what seemed like ages, but nobody moved or spoke. A gentle humming sound filled the room as the wand twirled steadily round and round, until at last it slowed ... and stopped. It was pointing at Lily.

"JEEPERS CREEPERS!" Lily jumped up and flung her arms around me. "AVA! That's completely and UTTERLY wonderful! You helped me when the wand chose you and now I can thank you!" She turned to Fairy Mary, her eyes shining. "It's OK, isn't it? If I let Ava decide who we're going to help today?"

Fairy Mary gave Lily a questioning look. "Are you sure? There's nobody you want to help?"

Lily shook her head. "Ava changed my life – she really did. I'm SO much happier now. PLEASE please let her choose!"

Fairy Mary McBee touched the Golden Wand. It gave a little jump, spun a couple of times, then stopped for a second time ... and this time it was pointing at me. Fairy Mary nodded. "The wand accepts Lily's decision."

"But it's not FAIR!" Melody growled. "Ava's had TWO turns!"

Jackson folded her arms. "She's right."

"No, she isn't." Fairy Mary's voice was quiet. "Lily has given Ava a gift." She gave them both a long cool stare.

Melody blushed and Jackson uncrossed her arms, wriggled in her seat, then stared at her fingers.

"I suppose it's OK," Jackson said at last. "Lily can do what she likes."

Fairy Mary turned to Melody. "Do you agree with Jackson, Melody?"

Melody shrugged. "Guess so."

"Thank you," Fairy Mary said, and she gave me and Lily a huge smile.

Chapter Six

Lily squeezed my hand as the shadows faded away and the room brightened. "Who are you going to help, Ava?"

"Café Blush," I said at once.

"A CAFE?" Melody gazed at me in astonishment.

"Well, it's really Little Val and Tallulah Sweet I want to help," I explained. "They run Café Blush, and they need more customers so they can pay the rent. If they can't pay the rent, they'll have to close down." I could feel tears pricking at the back of my eyes as I went on, "It's not just any café, you see. I don't know what the people who live in my flats would do without them. They're SO kind! They let old ladies have free cups of tea, and they keep an eye on the people who are a bit wobbly on their feet, and they take in parcels and pass on messages... Oh, they're at the very middle of everything!"

"They sound lovely," Emma said.

Jackson raised her eyebrows. "If they're so wonderful, why aren't they heaving with customers?"

"A new café's opened up the road," I said. "People must be going there instead."

"Does the new place sell nicer food?" Sophie asked.

I shook my head. "No. It's cheaper, but the cake is horrid and the sandwiches are always stale."

"So how do you want us to help?" Madison straightened her glasses. "Do we need to make cakes? I'm not much good at cooking."

"I can make ginger biscuits," Olivia offered.

Sophie looked doubtful. "They are a bit crunchy sometimes, Olivia. Nice, but crunchy."

Fairy Mary McBee stood up. "I'll leave you girls to decide what to do," she told us. "The Travelling Tower is ready for you, and if you need any help, Fairy Fifibelle, Miss Scritch and I will be in the sitting-room next door."

We watched the Fairy Godmothers walk away – well, Fairy Mary and Miss Scritch walked. Fairy Fifibelle Lee always glides.

"So," said Melody, folding her arms, "tell us what you're thinking, Ava."

"Um..." My mind was racing. What would be the best way to help Little Val and Tallulah?

"Will we be invisible?" Emma asked. "Or will they be able to see us?"

Madison fingered her necklace. "Eight girls arriving all at once is an awful lot. Besides, I haven't got any money.

I couldn't even buy a cup of tea."

"Nor me," Lily said.

"We'll tap our pendants and make ourselves invisible," I said. "I think we should look at the other café first and find out why people are going there, rather than to Café Blush."

Jackson nodded. "Maybe we can put their customers off. We could float their plates up in the air, then let them drop so they all smash to smithereens!"

Melody giggled. "Or put a Solidifying Spell on the sandwiches, so they're so heavy they can't be picked up."

"I don't think we ought to do that." Olivia sounded worried. "I mean, they're not trying to get people away from Café Blush on purpose, are they?"

Jackson and Melody looked at each

other. "Honestly, Olivia!" Jackson rolled her eyes. "You're no fun at all!"

Olivia blushed. "I'm sorry," she said.

Lily leant over and gave her a hug. "You're just kind. That's why we like you so much."

Melody pulled at Jackson's arm. "Let's make our own plan when we get there. We don't have to do the same as the others, do we?"

"Good thinking." Jackson gave Melody

a high five, and they grinned at each other before turning to me. "So, shall we head for the Travelling Tower, Ava?"

"Yes," I said. I wondered what Melody and Jackson might get up to, but decided to worry about that later. I asked if everyone had their necklaces on.

Madison winked at me, tapped her pendant ... and vanished.

"Can you see me?" It was Madison's voice, and she was laughing. If I screwed

up my eyes, I could see a very faint outline, but that was because I was a Stargirl. Nobody else would have known she was there.

Lily gave a long, happy sigh. "Isn't being a Stargirl FUN?" she said, and she tapped her pendant as well.

"Hang on a minute!" I stared at the empty space where I knew Lily was standing. "If you all turn invisible, I won't be able to see if everyone's got to the Travelling Tower. I don't want to leave anyone behind."

Madison and Lily laughed, tapped their pendants twice, and reappeared.

Chapter Seven

When we'd checked that our magic pendants were ready and in working order, we set off for the Travelling Tower. We had to walk through the sitting-room to get there, and we saw Fairy Mary, Fairy Fifibelle Lee and Miss Scritch sitting close together in front of the fire. They were having a really intense discussion and hardly looked up as we filed past. Fairy Fifibelle gave us a little wave, but that was all.

"I wonder what they're talking about?" Emma said.

A voice right beside us answered. "None of your business, young lady!"

We jumped and looked round. One of
the Fairy Godmothers was leaning out of
her picture and shaking her finger at us.
There are lots of portraits on the sitting-
room walls. Most of them are portraits of
the Fairy Godmothers who were at the
Academy long ago, when it was Cloudy
Towers. Madison and I love looking at
them, although some of them are rather
fierce – and the one who had spoken to
Emma is definitely the fiercest.

"Young girls!" She was positively
scowling. "I don't approve. I don't approve
at all! You're far too young to be scurrying
about on your own. I'll be keeping an eye
on you. Remember that!" And then she
popped back into her frame, and you'd
never ever have known she was anything
more than a picture.

"Goodness!" Emma looked SO surprised it made me giggle.

Madison was laughing too. "I do like the fact that they care about us, even if they are a bit scary."

"A BIT scary?" Emma's eyes were as round as saucers. "She's TERRIFYING!"

There was a muffled "TCHAH!" from

73

the picture, and Emma grabbed my arm.
"Come on! Let's go!"

The Travelling Tower, or the TT as we
sometimes call it, is a long way away from
our workroom. It's down a whole lot of dark
winding corridors, lit only by the tiniest
slit windows. Madison says she thinks the
corridors change from day to day, and she
might well be right. As we walked, I'm sure
I saw a corner straighten out in front of me.
We've never explored the whole Academy;
we just know that there are hundreds of
towers. The Travelling Tower is special,
though – it's like a glass-walled lift attached
to the end of the building, if you can imagine
that. If we want to travel anywhere, we get
inside. The cloud the Academy rests on
takes us to where we need to go, and then,

when we get there, the TT takes us up or
down, whichever we need.

Anyway, we were chatting about cake
and the kinds we liked best as we walked,
and that might be why we lost our way.
One minute I was absolutely certain the
Travelling Tower was just around the
corner, the next minute we were facing a
spiral stairway that none of us had ever
seen before.

"Oops," Lily said. "Does anyone know
where we are?"

None of us did.

"Maybe we should find our way back,
and start again," Emma suggested.

But when we tried, we couldn't do
that either. We went down the left-hand
corridor and we went down the right-

hand corridor, but every single time we found ourselves back in front of the same spiral staircase.

"I think we should go up it," Madison said. "It's obviously one of the towers. If we go to the top, we might be able to see where we are."

Olivia and Sophie looked doubtful, but Jackson and Melody leapt for the steps and started upwards. Emma and Madison began to follow them, but Lily hesitated. "Do you think it's OK?" she asked.

"It must be," I said. "Fairy Mary wouldn't have anything nasty here in the Academy, would she?"

"What if there's a really BAD Fairy Godmother?" Sophie asked. "Didn't Sleeping Beauty find a bad fairy at the top of a spiral staircase?"

"That was in a palace," I said, as firmly as I could. "Anyway, we should all stick together. Come on! We'll be fine. We can't keep walking round in circles for ever."

 77

Have you ever been up a spiral staircase? You can't see further than a very short way ahead and it feels like you're climbing for ever and ever. My legs were beginning to feel really wobbly when I heard a shout from up above. It was Melody, and she was yelling, "Hurry up! It's FABULOUS!"

We rushed to see where she was, all aches and pains forgotten.

Melody had found a door, and she and Jackson had wrestled it open. It led to an outdoor balcony that went right round the top of the tower, and as we tumbled out we could feel the wind blowing in our faces.

"Ohh," Olivia moaned, and she went pale. (She SO doesn't like heights!) She stood on the balcony trembling, with her eyes tightly shut. "It's too high," she whispered. "I don't want to look!"

Melody shook her head. "You're such a wimp, Olivia."

"She can't help it," I said, and I took Olivia's arm and helped her back to the top of the steps. "Don't worry," I told her. "And don't take any notice of Melody. We'll see if we can find out where we are, and then we'll go back."

I went to the edge of the balcony and looked over the rail, and I caught my breath. We were SO high up! I could only just make out the houses far, far below.

"WOW!" I breathed. "WOW!"

Lily was beside me. "We've never been this high before, have we? It's scary – but kind of fun, too."

"Yes," I agreed, "but I don't know how we're going to get to Café Blush..."

"LOOK!" It was Jackson. "There's the TT!

 79

It's right below us … and it's coming up!"

She was right. The Travelling Tower was making its way up the side of the building in a series of leaps and bounds.

"Do you think it's coming to collect us?" Madison asked. She sounded hopeful, and it was as if the TT heard her. It made a sudden rush and a moment later it was hovering alongside the balcony before linking on with a solid-sounding CLUNK!

 80

A small section of the balcony slid to one side, and there in front of us was a neat little railed ramp leading to the door of the Travelling Tower.

"Excellent!" Melody clapped her hands. "Everybody in!" She ran across the ramp ... and screamed.

Chapter Eight

Did I tell you that the TT has glass walls? There are glass walls all the way round, except for a section where there's a small control panel with buttons and levers. (That's how we make it go up and down.) The odd thing is that when you're inside, you can see out perfectly, but when you're outside, the glass often looks misty. I could tell there were two people inside, but I couldn't see who the second person was at first. When I did, I understood why Melody had been so surprised.

The Fairy Godmother from the picture in the sitting-room was standing in the lift with her picture frame hooked over her arm. She was telling Melody off for screaming. "REALLY, child! What a fuss! I knew you'd go the wrong way – all that chit-chat and no concentration – so I called Fairy Fifibelle Lee, and she was kind enough to pop me into the Travelling Tower. I've brought it up to meet you."

"B–b–but..." I'd never heard Melody stammer before. "But you're a PICTURE!"

The Fairy Godmother gave her a cool stare that reminded me of Miss Scritch. "And isn't it true that a good portrait captures the essence of a personality?"

"Erm..." Melody blinked. "I mean, yes."

The Fairy Godmother moved the frame to her other arm. "Well, there you are. You're observing the essence of Theodosia Placket. Of course, I can't do as much as I'd like to these days. A frame is SUCH a restriction!" She peered out at me. "As I understand it, you are leading today's expedition. Kindly inform me of your destination, and I'll set the course."

I couldn't help it; I had to rub my eyes. I could tell Theodosia Placket wasn't quite

real; there was a weird blurriness about her, as if I was looking through the wrong kind of spectacles. "We're going to Café Blush in Morning Street," I said.

The Fairy Godmother nodded. "Good. Now, hurry up. I can't bear dilly-dallying!"

Jackson, Madison, Lily and Emma walked across the ramp and into the Travelling Tower with no problem.

But Sophie hesitated. "What about Olivia? She'll never manage!"

I'd been thinking exactly the same thing. Olivia was still crouched in the doorway at the top of the stairs, her eyes tightly shut.

"Just leave her," Jackson called. "She can go down the stairs and back to the sitting room."

"No." I folded my arms. "Olivia's part

of Team Starlight and we look after each other."

Melody turned to Theodosia. "Can't you magic her over here?"

The Fairy Godmother looked horrified. "Certainly not! Fairy Mary McBee would be MOST upset. You girls must solve your problems yourselves."

Melody shrugged. "Ava! You're going to have to do something with Olivia!"

I looked at my friend. She was trembling, and I felt really sorry for her ... then I remembered, and felt so silly for not having thought of it before. The Sparkling Spell!

"Sophie," I said, "could you walk slowly into the TT? I'm going to see if I can use the Sparkling Spell on Olivia so she has to copy you."

Sophie nodded. "Good luck," she said, and she walked slowly and steadily along the ramp and into the Travelling Tower. I took a deep breath, and pointed my star finger at Olivia. "PLEASE let it work," I whispered … and a cloud of tiny sparkles came floating down and clung to Olivia's shoulders.

At once, she stood up. "Good luck," she said – and she sounded EXACTLY like Sophie! Then she walked slowly and steadily into the Travelling Tower without a moment's hesitation. Madison and Emma grabbed Olivia and hugged her as she stared round in astonishment, and rubbed her eyes as if she'd just woken up.

"I'm here!" Olivia said. "How did I do it? I was terrified!"

"Your friend helped you with a very effective Copying Spell." Theodosia Placket sounded approving. "But we should get going, don't you think?"

I nodded. "Yes, please." The Travelling Tower's doors closed and we began to float gently down. Melody and Jackson were whispering to each other in a corner,

but the rest of us stared out through the glass walls as we passed birds, then roof tops, and finally sank between two tall trees and came to rest above a dusty patch of grass.

"I know where we are!" I said. "We're on Tallulah's parking space. Come on, Stargirls! Let's save Café Blush!"

Emma, Lily and Madison tapped their pendants, and as they vanished Olivia and Sophie did the same. Melody and Jackson tapped theirs ... but nothing happened.

Jackson frowned. Melody looked puzzled. "Why isn't it working?"

Theodosia Placket made a sharp tut-tutting noise. "I'd have thought that was quite obvious. Did you help your friend Olivia? No. Did you encourage her? No.

In fact, if I remember correctly, you suggested she was left behind."

Jackson blushed, but Melody went pale.

"How can we get the magic back?" she asked.

"That is for you to find out." Theodosia heaved her picture frame up around her shoulders. "You young people are exhausting; I need a rest. When you return to the Stargirl Academy, please hang me back on the wall." And the stars that swirled round the Travelling Tower were so bright we had to cover our eyes.

Chapter Nine

When we opened our eyes Theodosia was gone, but in the corner of the Travelling Tower, leaning against the glass wall, was her portrait. It looked exactly as it did when it was hanging on the walls of the Academy sitting-room, except for one thing. Theodosia's eyes were shut.

"Wow," Emma said. "What do we do now?"

"We go and save Café Blush," I said.

"What about us?" Melody asked. It was strange. She and Jackson are usually so sure they know best that they don't ask our opinion about anything.

"I think we should go to the other café

92

first," I said slowly. "You and Melody can have a drink while we watch and listen. You could ask the owners why they've opened there. And if they've got any special plans..."

Jackson brightened. "No probs," she said. "And we'll find out what they think about your Café Blush."

"Good idea," I agreed, and we all walked out of the Travelling Tower and set off down the road. As we passed Café Blush, I saw there was nobody inside. Little Val was standing in the window. She looked up hopefully as Melody and Jackson walked towards the door, then drooped as they went past. I SO wanted to rush in and give her a massive hug and tell her we were trying to help her, but I stopped myself. Instead I followed Melody and

Jackson. I knew Team Starlight was beside me – Madison and Lily were chatting, and Emma was giggling with Sophie and Olivia.

We could hear the noise from the new café long before we got there. It was heaving! There were tables and chairs on the pavement outside, and there wasn't a

single empty seat. A man and a woman were whizzing about, handing out teas and coffees and plates of cake and buns. For a moment, I thought they must be having a private party, but then the man saw Melody and Jackson. "Hi there! I'm Kyle! Welcome to the Crazy Cancan Café! Haven't seen you here before – come in!

We'll fit you on the bench inside, and you must have a free fizzy drink!"

The man led Melody and Jackson inside the café and showed them to a tiny bench behind a rickety table. There were a whole load of mums and babies sitting on the other side, and there was hardly room for me and Emma to squeeze in and stand behind them. Lily, Madison and Sophie stayed by the doorway; I could just make out that they were there. I couldn't see Olivia.

One of the mums leant across to Melody. "Have you been here before? It's an AMAZING deal! Every time you come, you get your loyalty card stamped and twenty stamps means the café will let your kids have their birthday party here for free!"

Another mum nodded. "So we all come

 96

every day ... even though the cake isn't
as nice as the cake in Café Blush."

Kyle had just come back with two
bright orange fizzy drinks, and he heard
her. "You don't like our cake, Julie? Ho ho
ho! What a joke!" But he didn't sound the
least little bit amused, and his eyes were
chilly.

Julie laughed. "Well, it IS a bit stodgy,

Kyle. Couldn't you make a chocolate cake like Little Val's? It's SO delicious!"

Kyle gave another false laugh. "Ho ho! Sal and I will have to see what we can do! We can't have unhappy customers at the Crazy Cancan Café, can we?" He slammed the fizzy drinks in front of Melody and Jackson, and marched off. A moment later, I saw him whispering to Sal. I began to edge my way over so I could hear what they were saying ... and I knocked against the next table where two teenage boys were sitting, and their drinks went flying.

"Oops! Sorry," I said – and only realised what I'd done when they stared round, looking to see where my voice had come from.

"WHAT...?"

Jackson jumped to her feet. "That was me! My foot slipped – I'm so sorry! Here, – have our drinks! We haven't touched them! Honestly!" And she grabbed her and Melody's glasses of orange fizz and plonked them down.

Luckily, the boys didn't work out that

Jackson would have needed legs three-metres long to reach them. They took the drinks, and Melody mopped up the mess with a couple of paper napkins. I breathed a sigh of relief and made my way to the back of the café. Kyle and Sal were talking in urgent undertones, but as I arrived Sal picked up a tray of coffees. I only just managed to get out of her way;

if I'd been any fatter, there'd have been a complete disaster.

Kyle was muttering to himself as he put some cash in the till. "Three weeks – that should do it. Just another flippin' three weeks of this and we'll be home and dry!" He slammed the till drawer shut and headed off to take more orders, and I had to do another mad leap.

"Hey! Ava!" It was Emma whispering in my ear. "Come outside! I've just heard something dreadful!"

I wasn't sorry to follow Emma out of the café. It was cramped and hot, and there was a weird smell of cooking oil. The tablecloths were dirty, too – it couldn't have been more different from my lovely Café Blush.

Madison and the others were waiting

for us outside. "Shall I get Melody and Jackson?" Lily asked.

I peered in through the café window. The Stargirls were deep in conversation with the teenage boys, and from the look on Jackson's face they were hearing something they didn't like. Without thinking I tapped on the glass, and all four of them looked up. The two boys blinked, frowned and turned to Melody. It was SO obvious they were asking her if she knew what had made the tapping noise; I saw her shake her head and do her best to look puzzled. Then she and Jackson got to their feet.

"AVA!" Madison was laughing so much she could hardly speak. "You can't do things like that!"

"I don't think I'm very good at being

invisible," I apologised. "I keep forgetting. It's lucky for me that Jackson was so quick-thinking – did you see what she did?"

"Yes," Olivia said. "And, look! Here they come!"

Olivia was right. Jackson and Melody were strolling out of the café, but the boys were following them. As they walked towards us, the older boy caught at Jackson's arm.

"Oi!" he said. "Don't walk off!"

Jackson gave him a cold stare. "We've got to meet our friends."

"Our dad's caff not good enough for you, then?" the boy sneered. "Spill our drinks, mess up the floor, then ask us loads of questions? What are you after?"

"Expect they're spies." The younger

boy rolled his eyes. "Posh girls like them. From that ickle pretty Slushy Blushy Café down the road. Well, guess what? It won't—"

"Shut up, Mick!" The older boy stuck his elbow into his brother's side. "SHUT UP!"

"Shut up, yourself," Mick said. The next minute, the two brothers were rolling on the pavement, kicking and punching.

"Come on," I said, and grabbed Jackson's hand. It was HOT! I looked down, and

her star finger was glowing bright red. "OH!" I said. "Quick! Tap your pendant!"

Jackson gave a squeak of excitement – and a moment later she was invisible. Melody tapped her own pendant as the boys pulled themselves back to their feet, and she vanished too. We held our breath as the boys looked first one way, then the other.

"Where did they go?"

"Dunno. Stupid girls." Mick made a face. "But they were up to something. All those questions…"

His older brother shrugged. "Won't make any difference. Dad's got it sorted. He says we'll be at Café Blush by the end of the month!"

Mick snorted. "Café Blush? It's going to be The Old Hippy Chippy! Won't be any fancy cakes there then."

Chapter Ten

As the boys walked back to the Crazy Cancan Café, we slipped around the corner and gave our pendants a double tap so we could see each other. It's difficult to have a serious conversation when you can't see who you're talking to.

"What did they mean?" I asked.

Emma sighed. "That's what I was going to tell you. The horrible man and the horrible woman were talking by the till. They're promising all these parties and treats so customers keep coming, but as soon as Little Val and Tallulah Sweet give up Café Blush, they're going to close the Crazy Cancan Café and move there, because it's bigger. And they WON'T give any of the free parties they've promised, because they're going to make Café Blush a chip shop."

"Emma's right." Melody was behind me. "Those boys were boasting about it. The landlord's already promised their dad the lease if Little Val and Tallulah can't pay their rent."

"I bet he doesn't know how horrible Kyle and Sal are," Lily said with feeling.

"The kitchen's horrible too." It was Olivia, and we turned to look at her. She's so quiet, but so surprising!

"I went to look, and it's disgusting. The floor's all sticky, and they've got heaps of dirty plates, and there are beetles on the shelves."

"YUCK!" Sophie made a face.

 107

But Madison began to chuckle. "Brilliant!" she said. "Well done, Olivia! Go and get them, Ava. You're much the best at the Copying Spell, and there's no room in that café for all of us."

"What?" I stared at her.

"Get the customers into the kitchen!

Once they see what it's like, they won't care how many parties they've been promised. Trust me!" Madison's eyes were gleaming behind her spectacles.

"You're right," Melody said. "Go on, Ava! You can do it!"

"I'll come with you," Jackson said, and she grinned at me. "You might knock something over."

I smiled back. "You were really clever. Thank you. And, yes. Let's do it together."

"I'll come too," Emma said. "You might need back-up."

We tapped our pendants so we were invisible again, and set off for the Crazy Cancan Café. The boys were leaning against the door, but we slid past without them noticing. A moment later we were back in the middle of all the mums and dads and grannies and babies, and squeezing between tables until we reached the kitchen door. Kyle and Sal were hurrying here and there, smiling their fake smiles and handing out their loyalty cards promising parties.

"How are we going to get people into the kitchen?" Jackson whispered.

"I don't know," I said, but at that moment a jug of orange skidded across a table and tipped straight into an old lady's lap.

"Emma!" I thought. "That has to be Emma!"

"Oh! Oh! Oh!" The old lady was drenched. "Fetch me a cloth! I'm soaked!"

"Of course, darling – be with you in a sec!" Kyle gave her a cheery wave, and headed for the kitchen.

As soon as he reappeared with a handful of grubby tea towels, I pointed my star finger at the small boy nearest me. "Do the same," I murmured under my breath. "PLEASE copy him!" And the boy stood up. He didn't see the sparkles in the air above his head; he headed straight for the kitchen.

"Robbie! ROBBIE!" his mum yelled, but Robbie took no notice.

Robbie's mum rushed after him ... and her scream told me she was in the kitchen. Two of her friends hurried to see what was going on, and they screamed too.

"Ladies! Ladies!" Kyle was flapping his

hands. "No one's allowed in the kitchen!"

"It's REVOLTING!" Robbie's mum had reappeared, Robbie wriggling in her arms and clutching a tatty tea towel. "And to think we've been eating here, day after day! I'm never coming back. NEVER!"

"Nor me!" It was another woman. She looked round at the other customers who were frozen in their seats, open-mouthed. "This place is a HEALTH HAZARD! There are beetles on every single surface! I'm going to report it to the authorities right now." And she stormed out, her face very red.

After that, it was complete madness. The adults in the café all fought their way into the kitchen, and they all came out looking furious. Some of them were clutching tea towels, and I guessed

Jackson and Emma had been casting Copying Spells too.

Two minutes later, the Crazy Cancan Café was empty, apart from Kyle, Sal and the two boys. Kyle was sitting at a table, his head in his hands, and Sal was shouting at him.

"It's time to go," Jackson whispered in my ear.

I agreed with her. I don't know what she did to Mick and his brother as we left, but they both let out a loud howl and began frantically rubbing their noses. I thought the café's customers would be outside, but they weren't. They were walking briskly down the road as if they knew exactly where they were going ... and they did.

By the time Jackson and I reached Café

Blush there wasn't a seat left, not even at the table where Melody was sitting, totally visible and looking like a cat who'd swallowed the cream.

As we stared, Melody beamed at Little Val and ordered herself a huge slice of chocolate cake.

"It was Melody's idea." Madison was

beside me. "She made herself visible and as she walked down here we put the Copying Spell on as many people as we could manage!"

"Genius," I said, and I meant it. "Hey! Why don't we go round the corner, make ourselves visible, then come back to celebrate? We could ALL have cake!"

"Hurrah!" Lily and Sophie banged me on the back and we scooted round the corner to where we'd left the Travelling Tower ... and stopped dead.

The TT was hovering above the ground and Fairy Fifibelle Lee was inside chatting happily to Fairy Theodosia Placket. Even though we hadn't tapped our pendants she could see us, and she waved.

"Darling girls! It's time to go! Hop in – you've only got a few minutes left!"

116

We must have looked as disappointed as
we felt, because Fairy Fifibelle gave us a
sympathetic smile. "I'm so sorry. Were
you having a wonderful time?"

"We were going to have cake," I said,
and she laughed.

"I'm sure we can find some cake back at

the Academy. Now, somebody's missing. Where's Melody?"

"I'll fetch her," I said, and before Fairy Fifibelle could stop me, I ran back round the corner. Melody was chatting to Little Val and Tallulah as she paid her bill.

"It's a LOVELY café," I heard her say. "My friend Ava told me it was brilliant, and she's right."

Little Val beamed at her. "You're a friend of Ava's? Our special girl? Will you be seeing her soon? I can't wait to tell her how busy we are. We've been SO worried, but I really think we're going to be fine."

Melody grinned. "I'll tell Ava. She'll be thrilled."

Chapter Eleven

Fairy Fifibelle Lee was right. When the TT whizzed us back to Stargirl Academy, we found that Fairy Mary had a wonderful meal ready for us, and we were allowed to eat it in the sitting-room in front of the fire. I saw that Theodosia Placket was back in her usual place; she gave me a tiny little wink as I walked past her.

"Well done, Stargirls," Fairy Mary said. "You had a difficult day today, but you did well." She looked at Melody and Jackson. "And I believe that you two have learnt a lesson."

Melody nodded, but Jackson sighed.

"I can be pretty horrible sometimes," she said. "I don't really mean it, though. It just seems to happen." Olivia was sitting next to her and Jackson gave her hand a squeeze. "Sorry for giving you a hard time."

"Well said, Jackson!" I'd never seen Miss Scritch looking so pleased. "It's very important to remember that some of us don't find it easy to be cheery and friendly all the time. We're all made in different ways."

"Quite right!" The voice echoed from across the room.

"Thank you, Theodosia dear." Fairy Mary stood up and shook the crumbs off her skirt. Scrabster wagged his tail. "But now, my wonderful Stargirls, it's time for you to go home. Ava, my dear, you can go through the Academy's front door – and here's something for you."

I took the piece of paper and looked at it. It was the recipe for the lovely coffee cake.

"Thank you!" I said. "Thank you so very much!"

I hugged all my friends, then walked to the door. As I opened it, I was caught up in a swirl of thick mist ... but I knew what to do. I took a deep breath, walked forward ... and found myself on the stairs outside my flat.

At once, I thought of Little Val and Tallulah Sweet. What were they doing? Had we really sorted out their problems for them?

I jumped down the last few steps and hurtled out of the street door. Into Café Blush I dashed – and it was full! Absolutely stuffed! And Little Val came running to give me a huge hug.

"Guess what?" she said. "That place up the road is going to be closed down. I've just heard. Health and safety!"

"Hurrah!" I said. "That's absolutely WONDERFUL news!"

Little Val nodded. "Isn't it?" And then she saw my pendant. In my hurry, I'd forgotten to hide it under my T-shirt. "That is SO pretty, Ava. Come and look, Tallulah!"

Tallulah came over to see. "That's BEAUTIFUL! Four of those lovely little stars look exactly as if they're lit up from the inside!"

"Four?" I said, and I had a look myself. "Oh ... oh, yes. So they are!" And I gave Little Val and Tallulah the biggest hug ever. I was SO happy for them — and I was happy for me too.

Four stars shining. Only two to go and then ... THEN I'd be a Stargirl!

Ava's Maze

We need to get to the
Travelling Tower.
Can you help us?

START

FINISH

Go to
www.stargirlacademy.com
to download a
FREE POSTER
of your favourite
Stargirl

Answer

Ava Chan

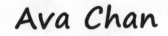

Loves:
Coffee cake

Hates:
Burnt baked beans

Good at:
Drawing

Starsign:
Sagittarius

Favourite colour:
Green

Dreams of:
Being less clumsy!